Welcome to Nerd Designs Press! Our goal is to provide you with exceptional designs that cater to your diverse interests. With our team of experienced art designers, we hope you thoroughly enjoy our captivating collection of books.

As a family-owned and operated business, we established ourselves in 2023 fueled by a deep-rooted passion for creating products that foster shared experiences among individuals and families. Today, we take immense pride in serving customers worldwide and sharing our unwavering enthusiasm with you.

We invite you to explore and delight in our wide range of products. Stay up to date with our latest book releases by signing up for our mailing list, or if you have a concept for a customized book, please visit our website by scanning the provided QR code. We would be thrilled to assist you in transforming your dream into a tangible reality.

If you have any questions or comments to enhance our products, please don't hesitate to reach out to us at nerddesigns@nerddesigns.org. We are here to assist you and ensure your utmost satisfaction.

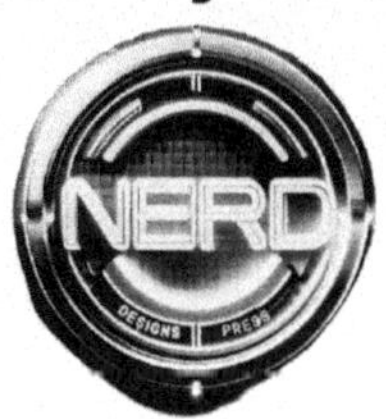

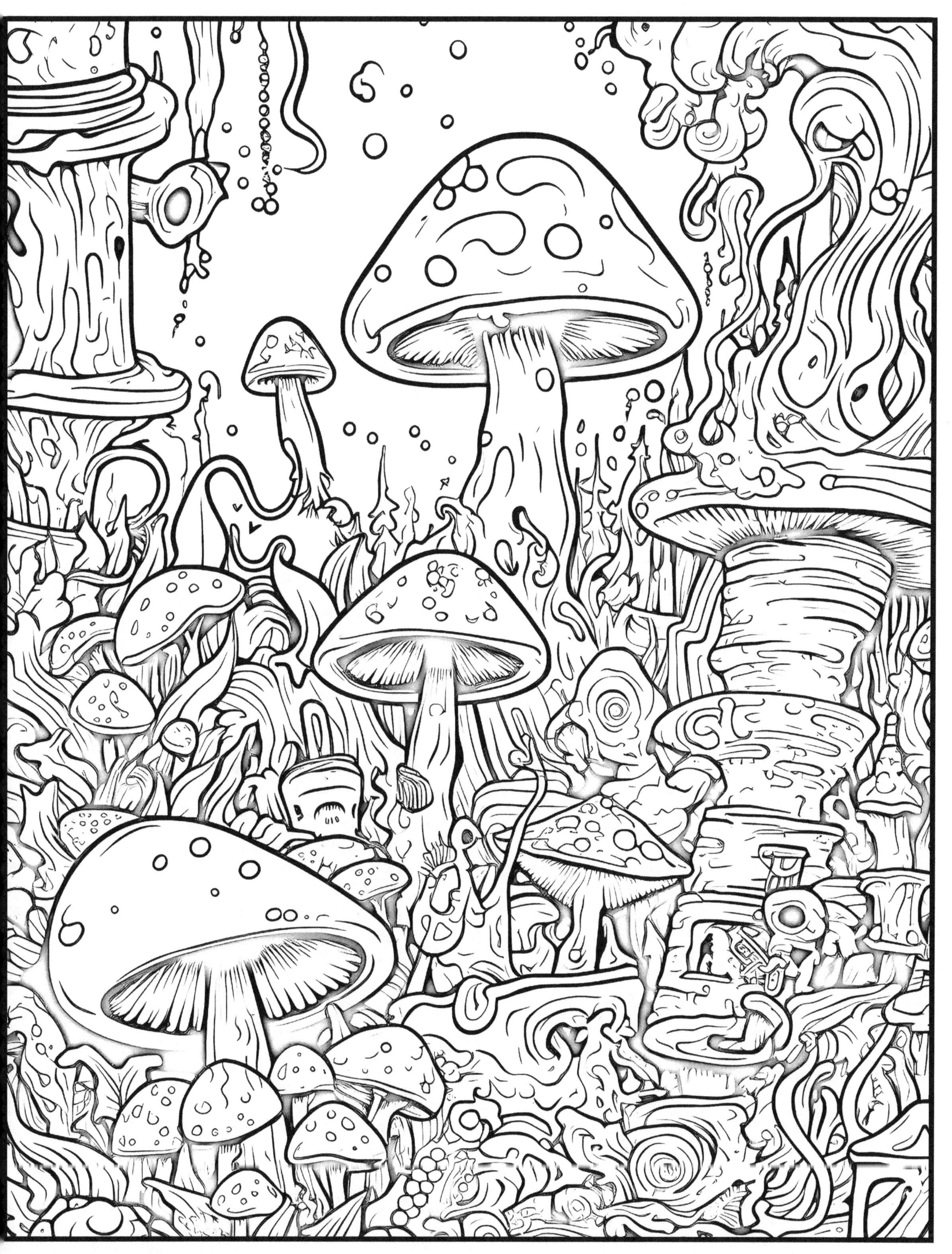

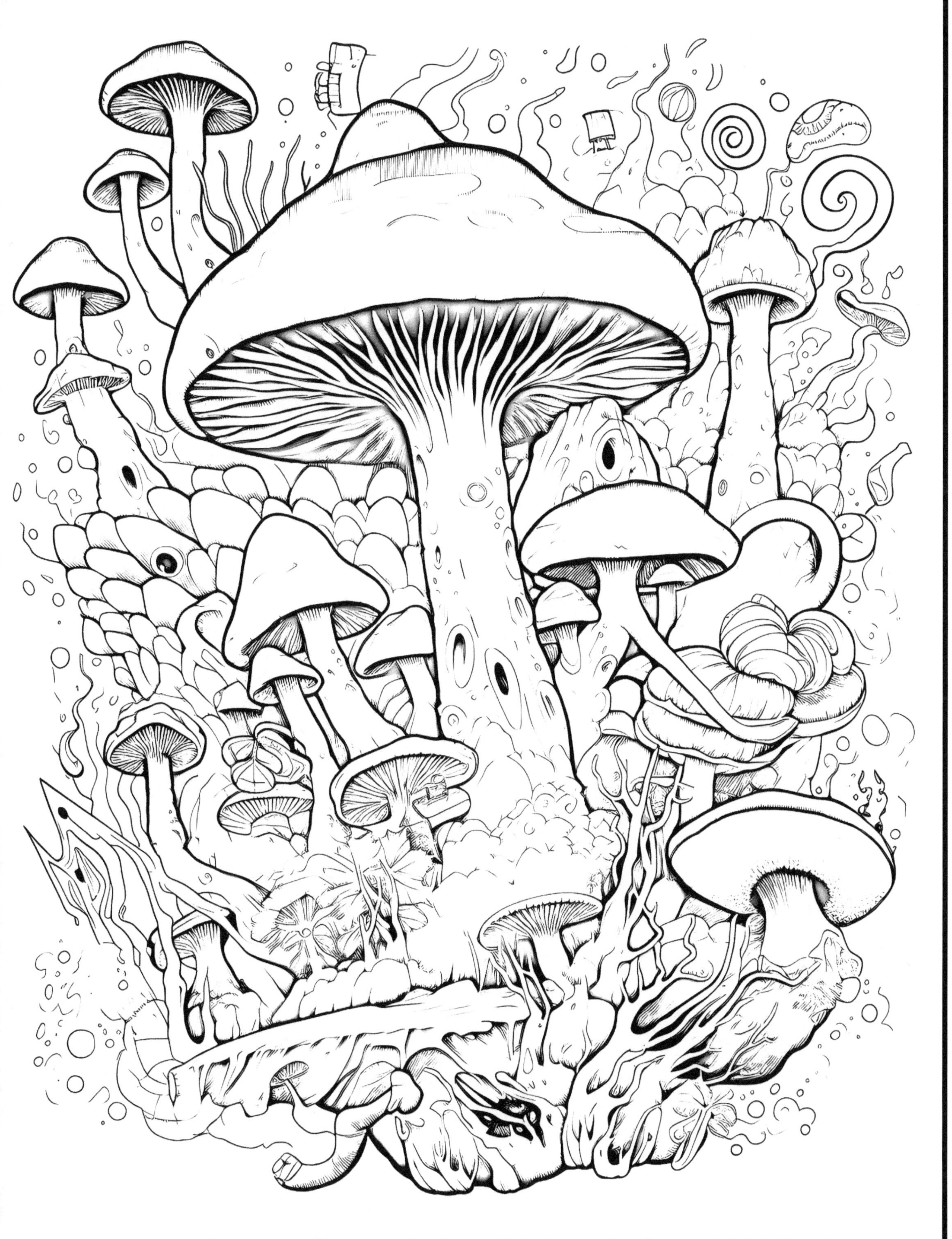

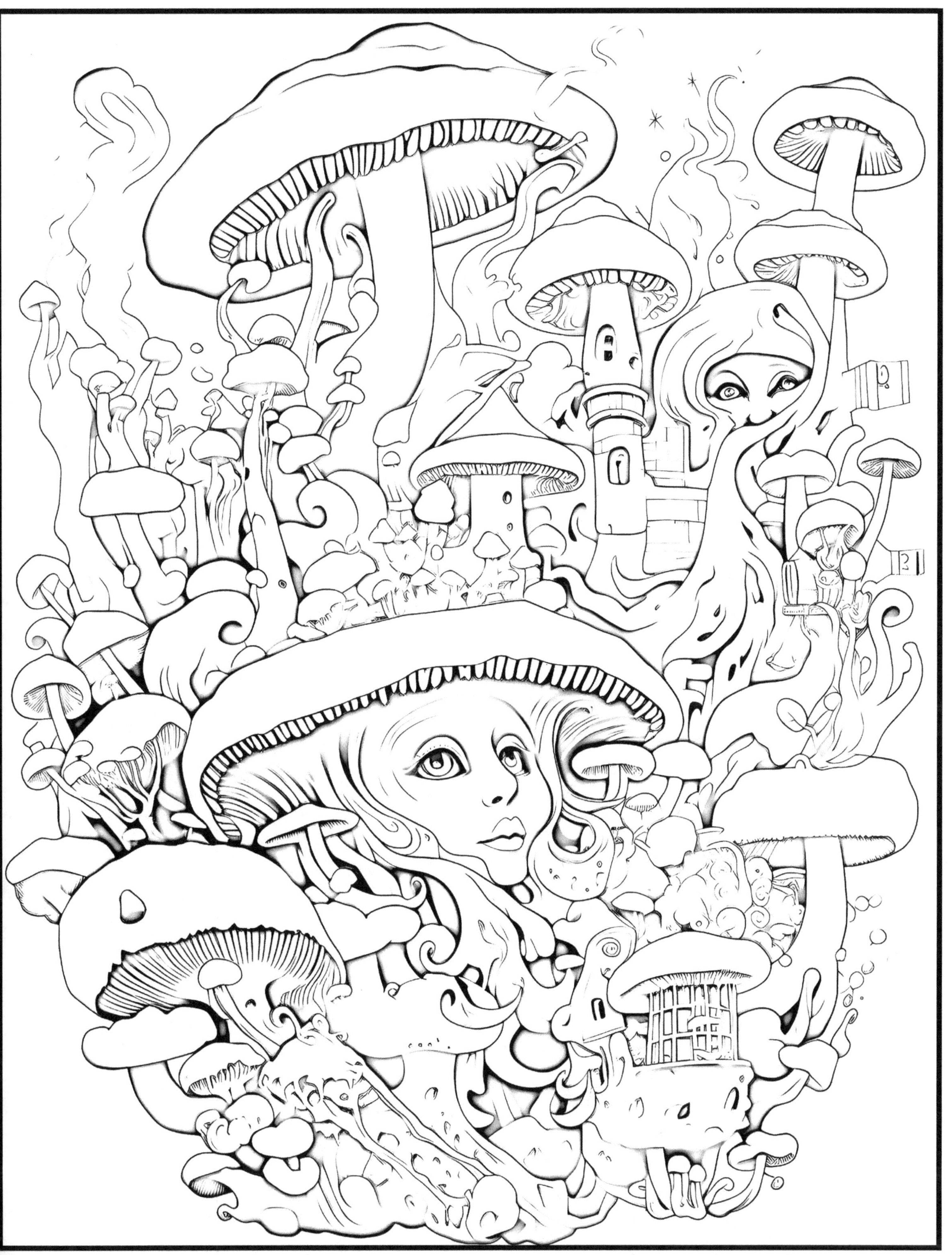

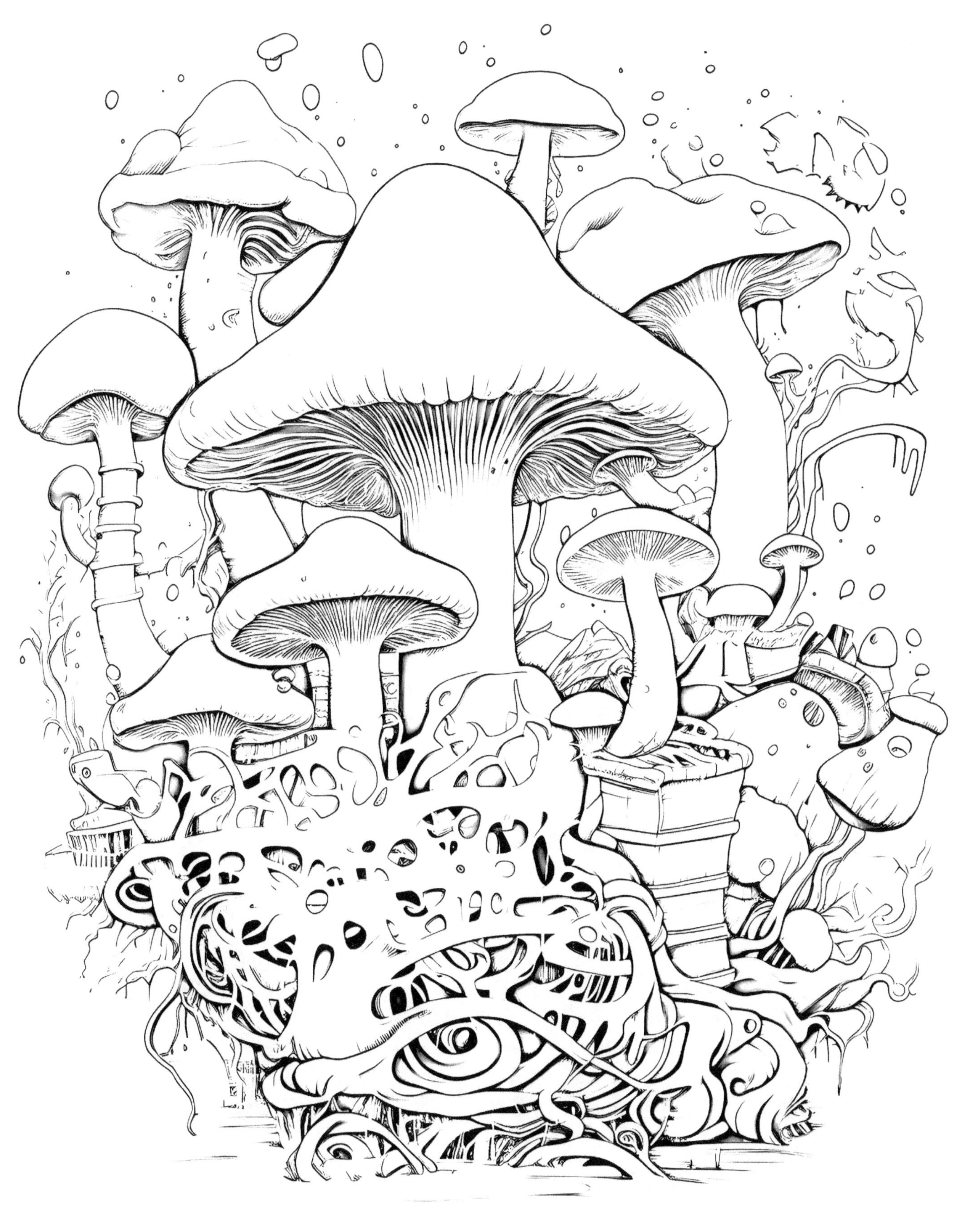

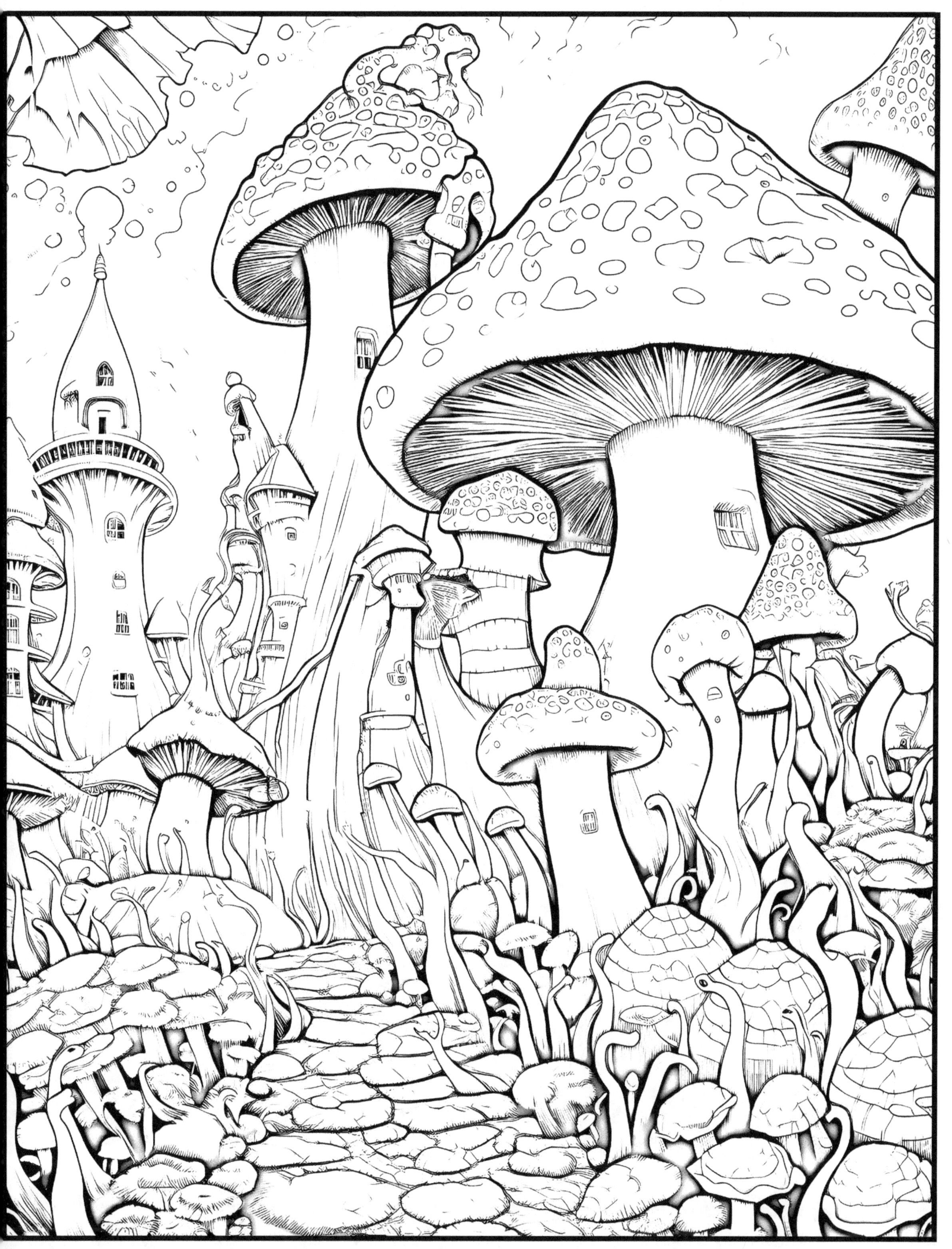

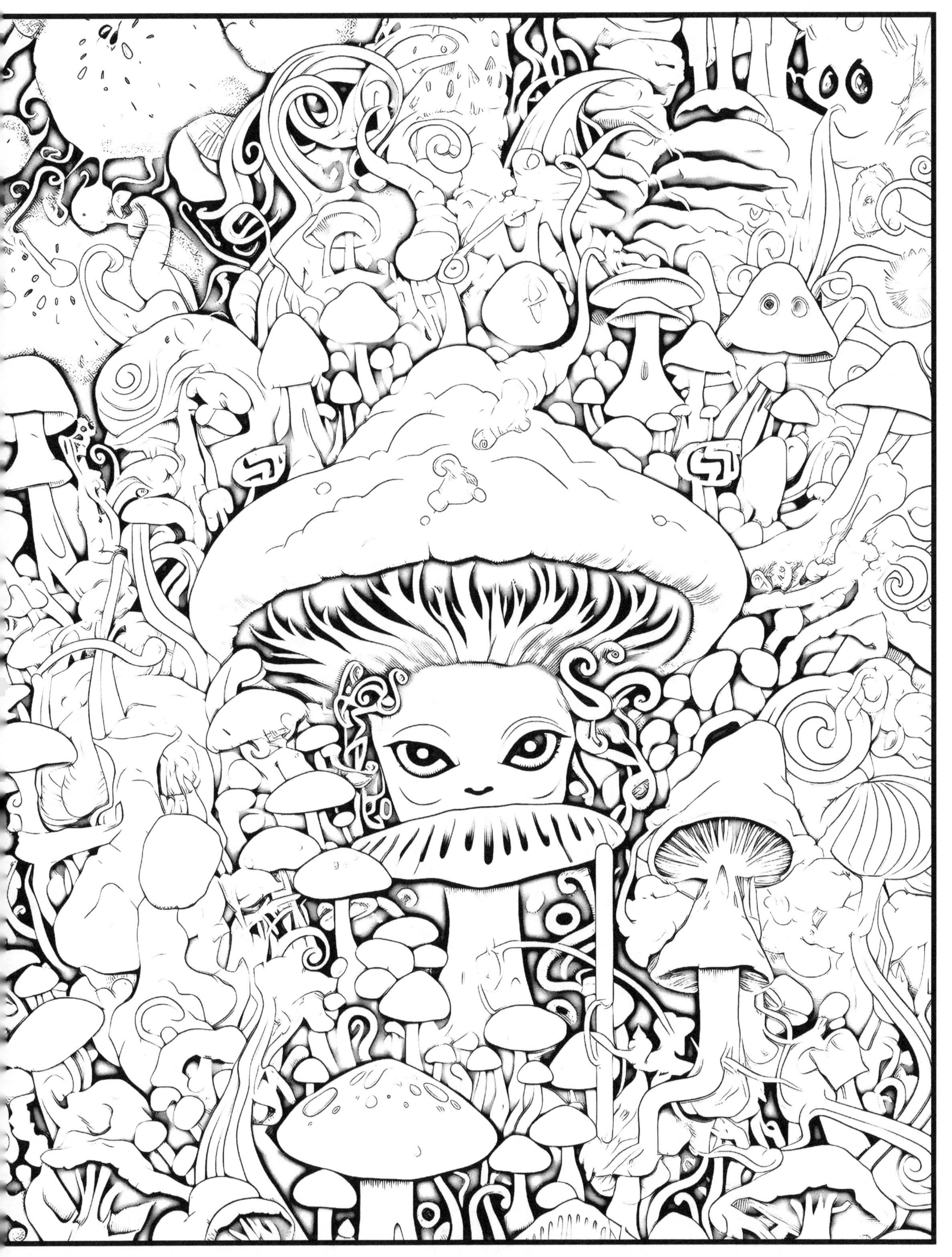

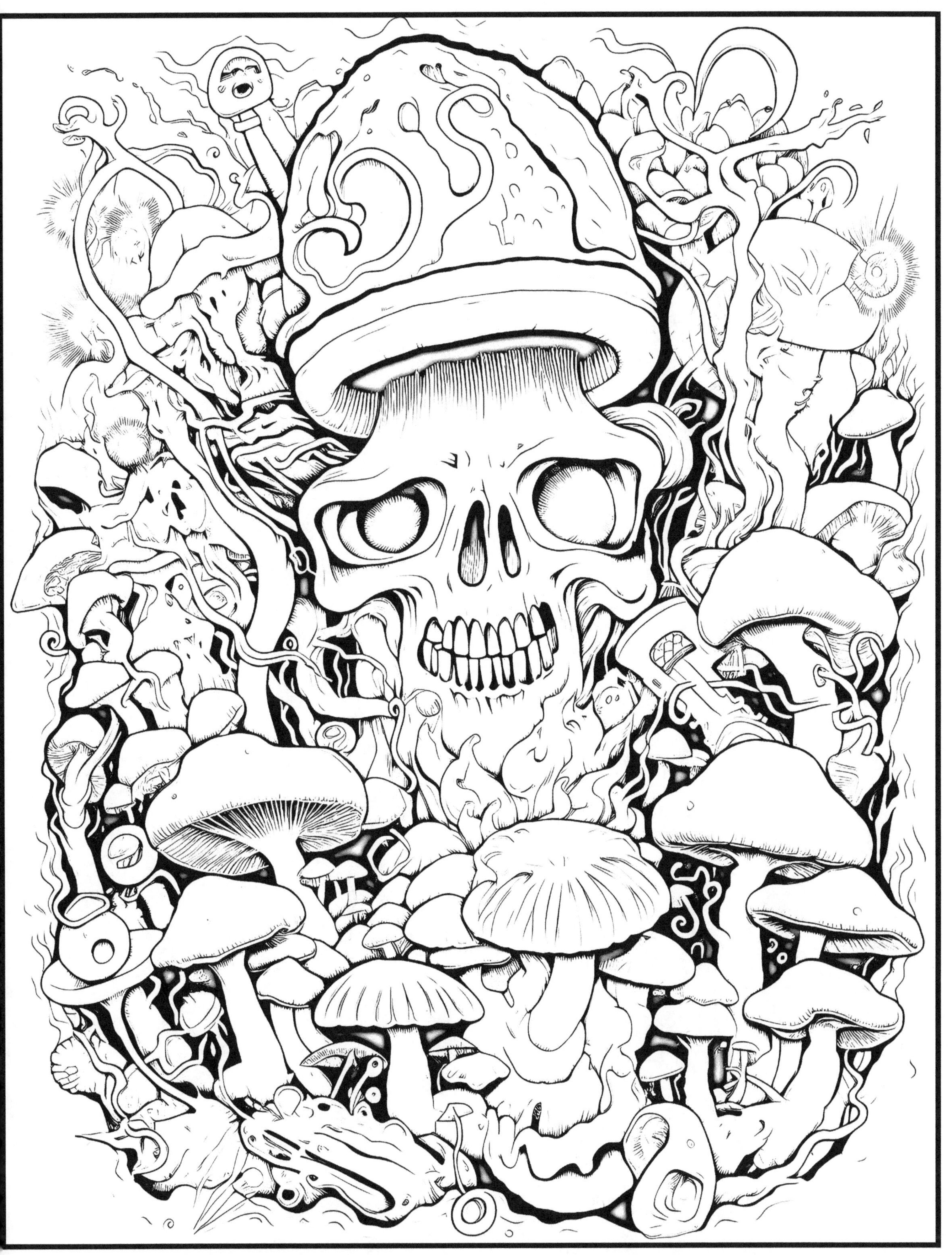

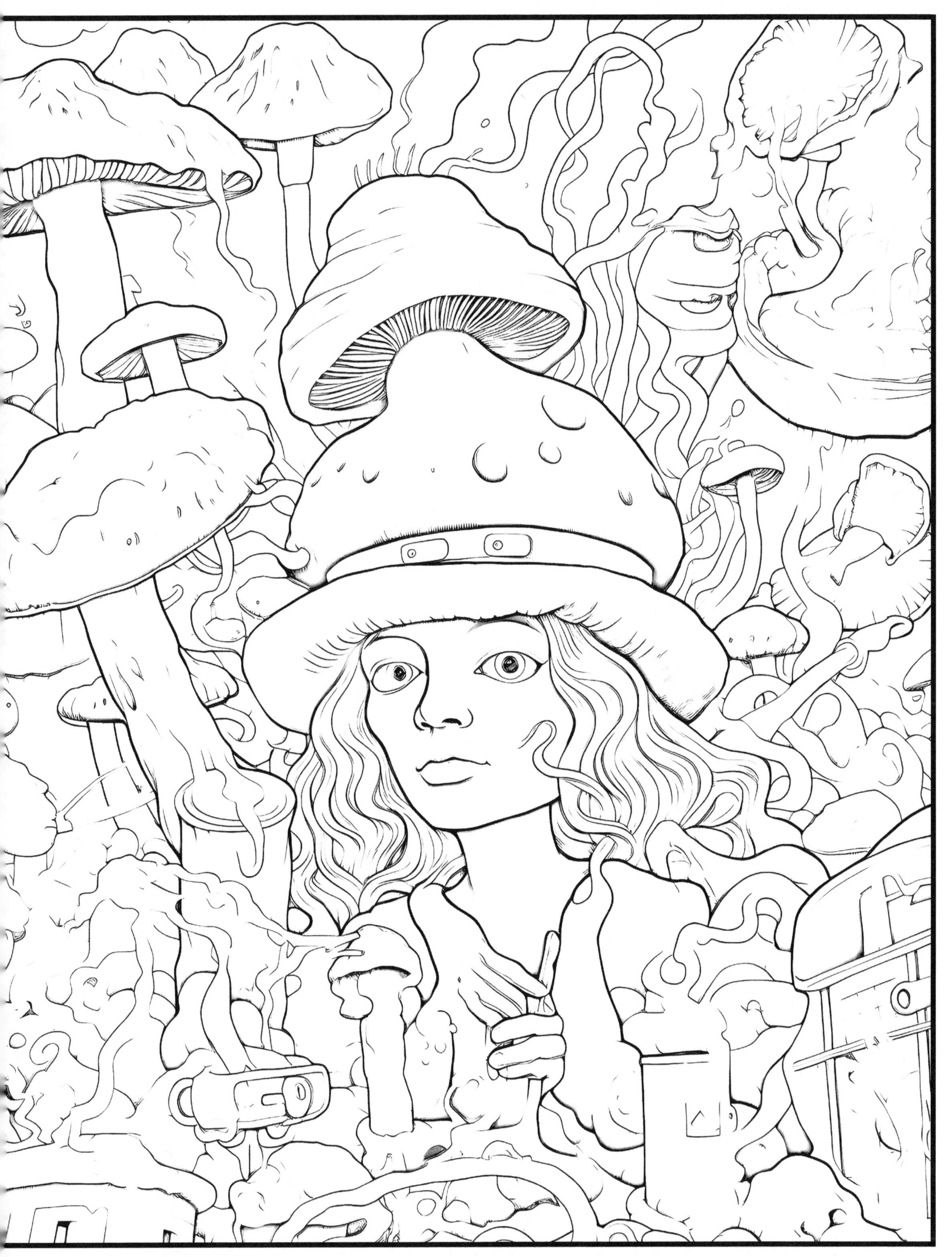

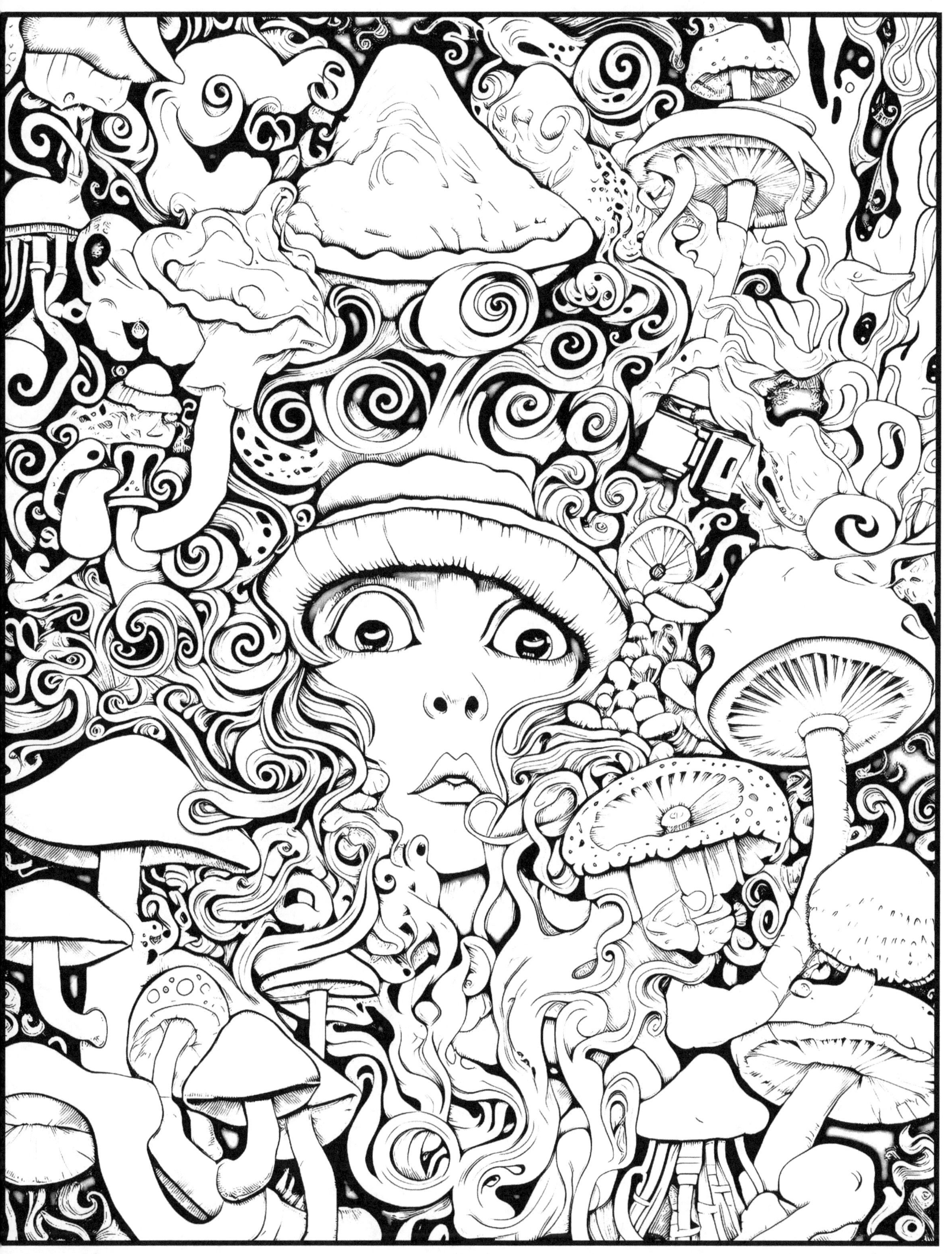

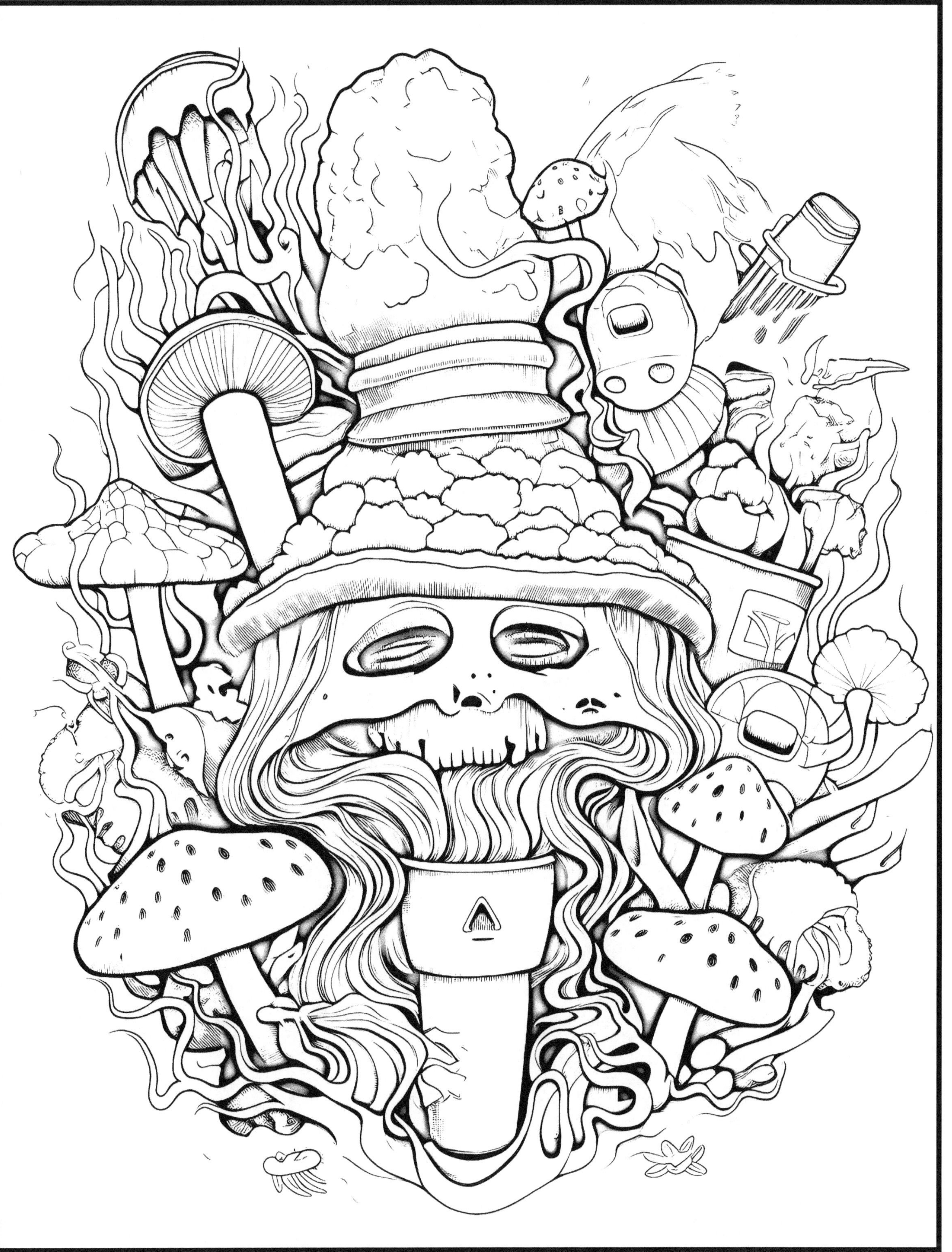

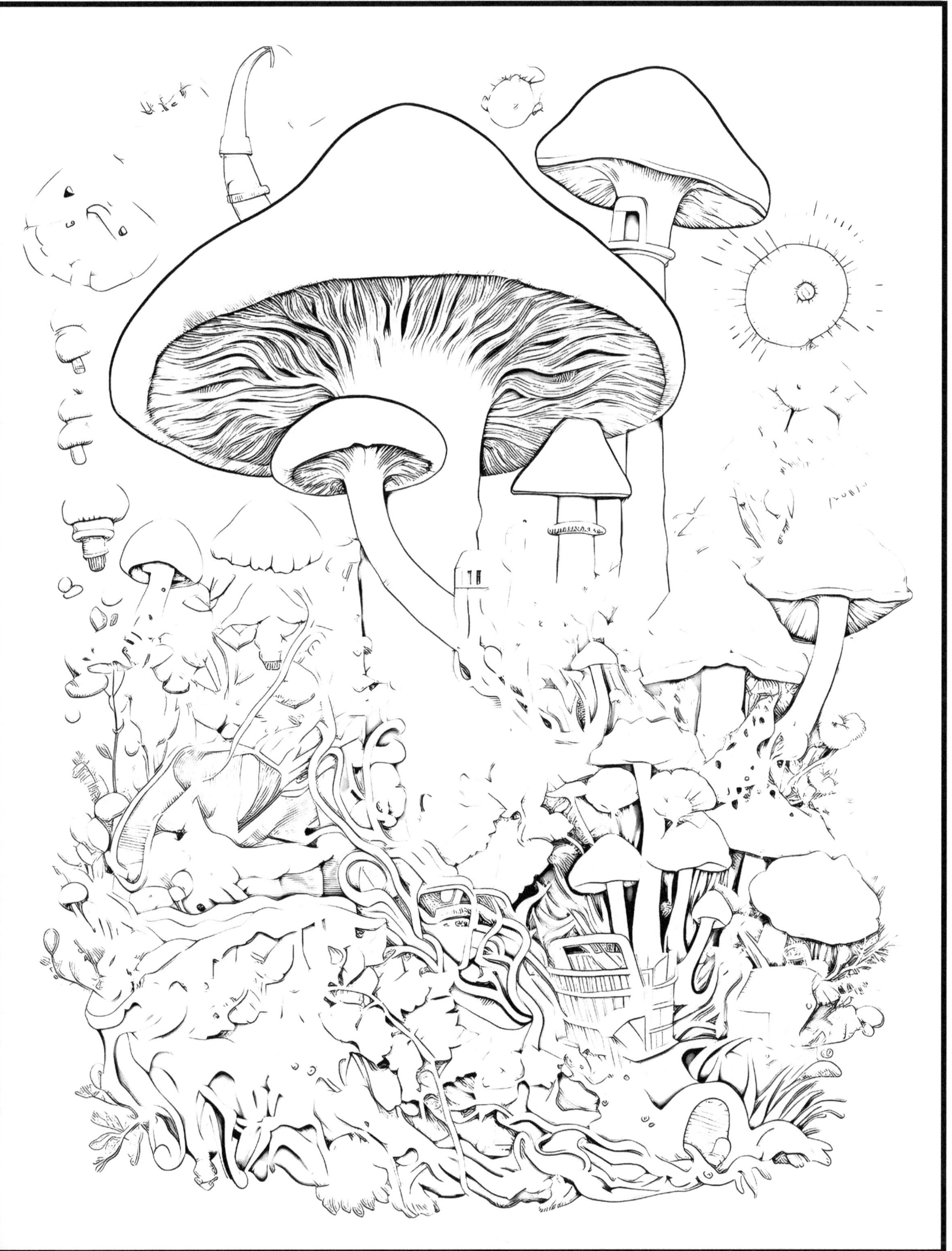

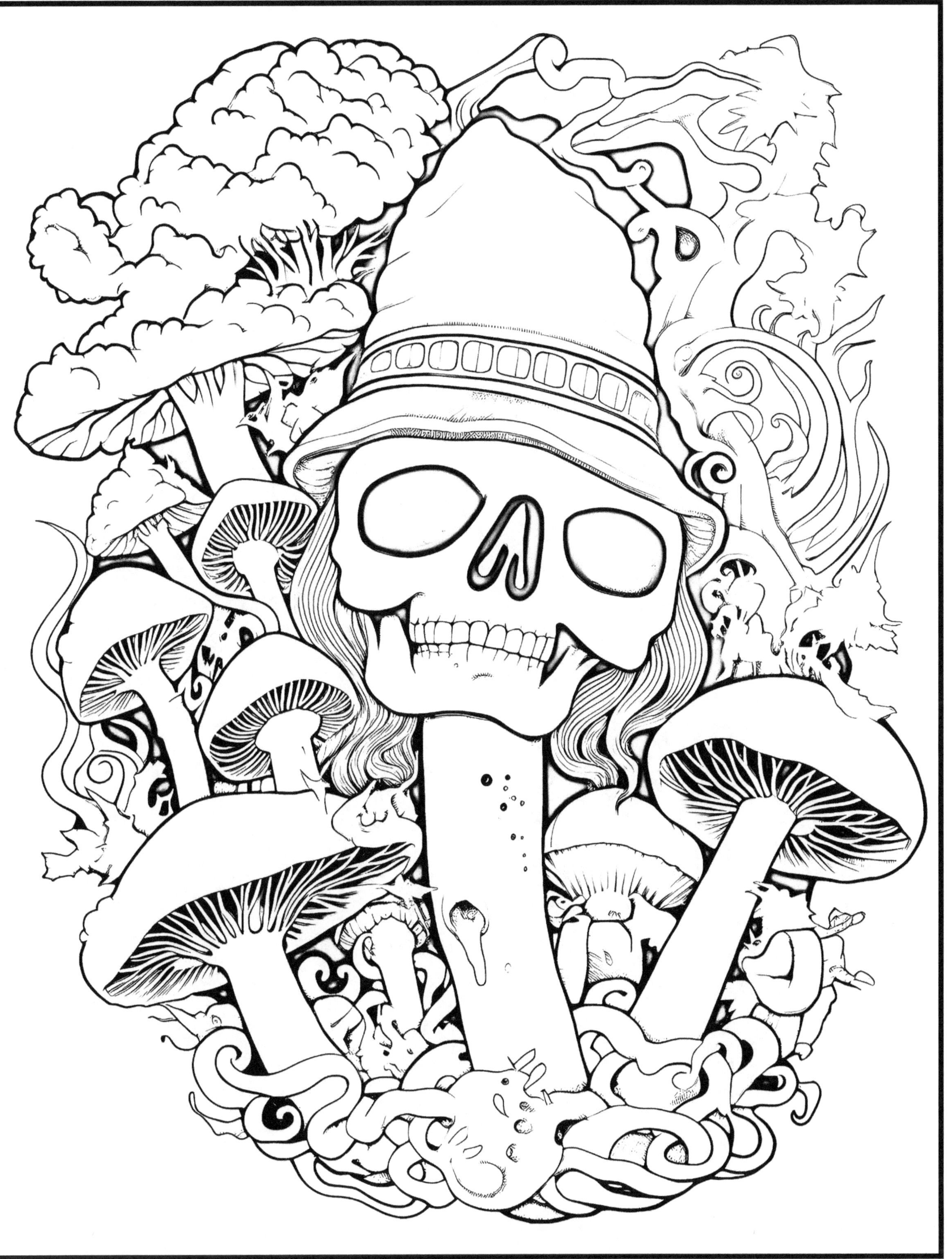

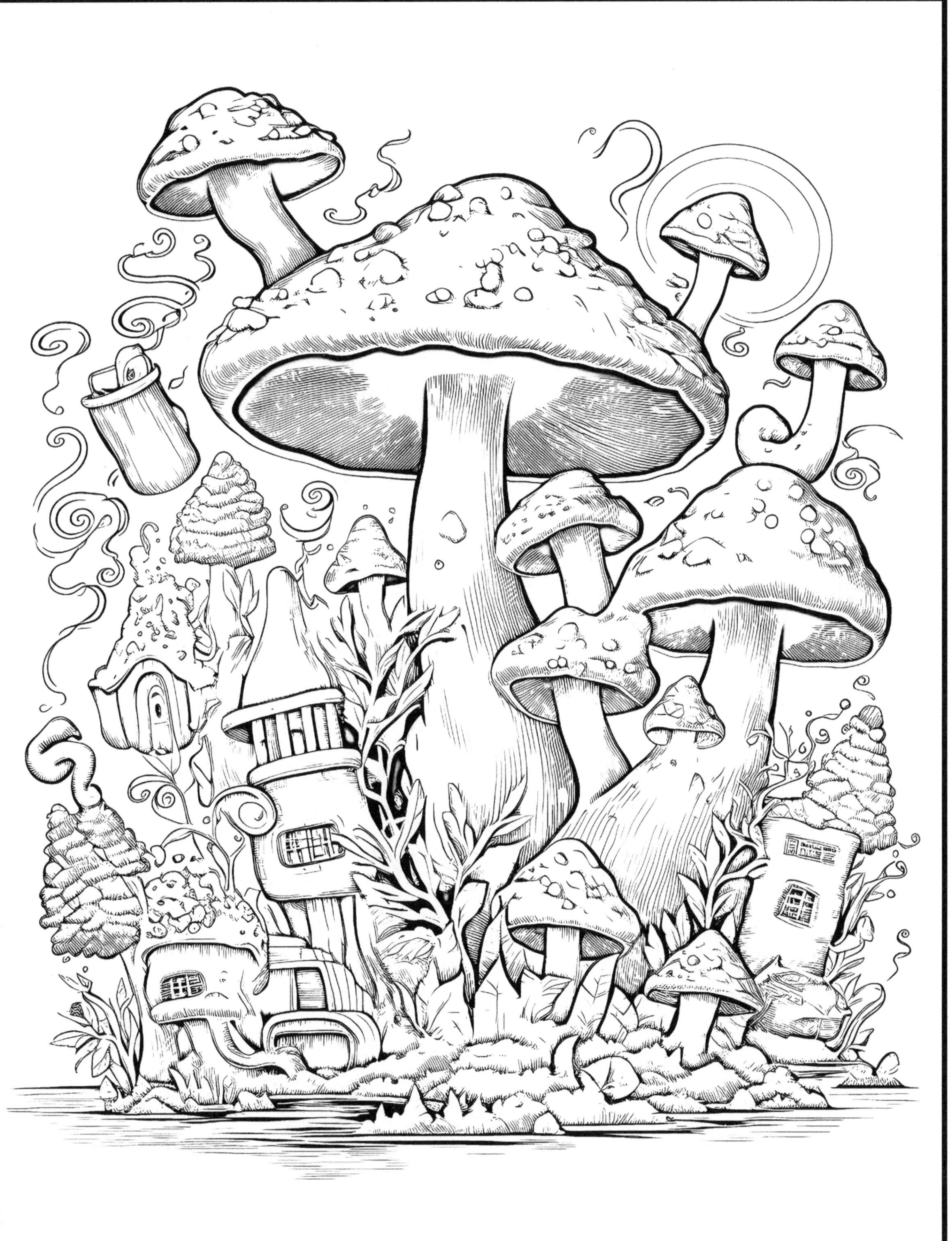

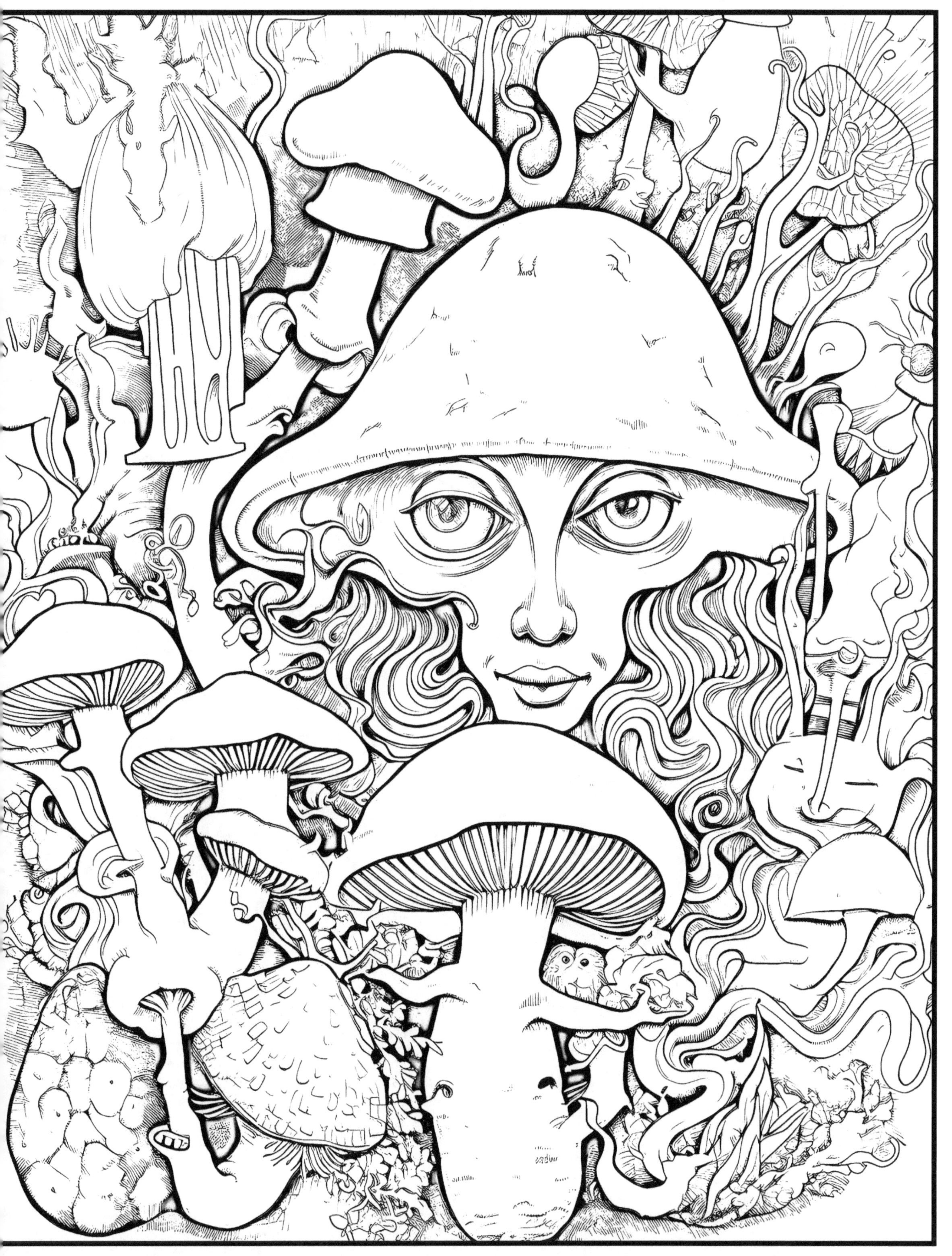

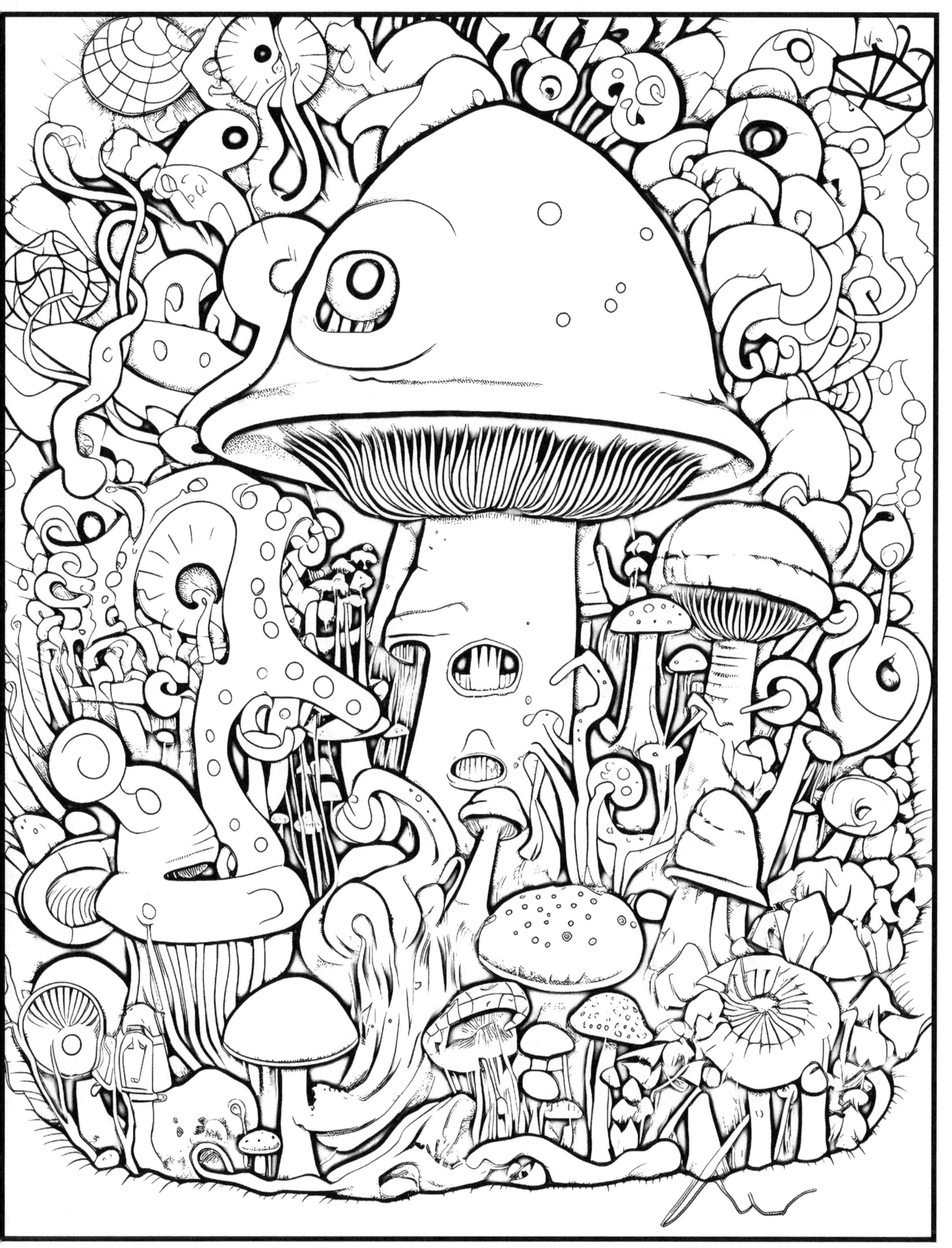

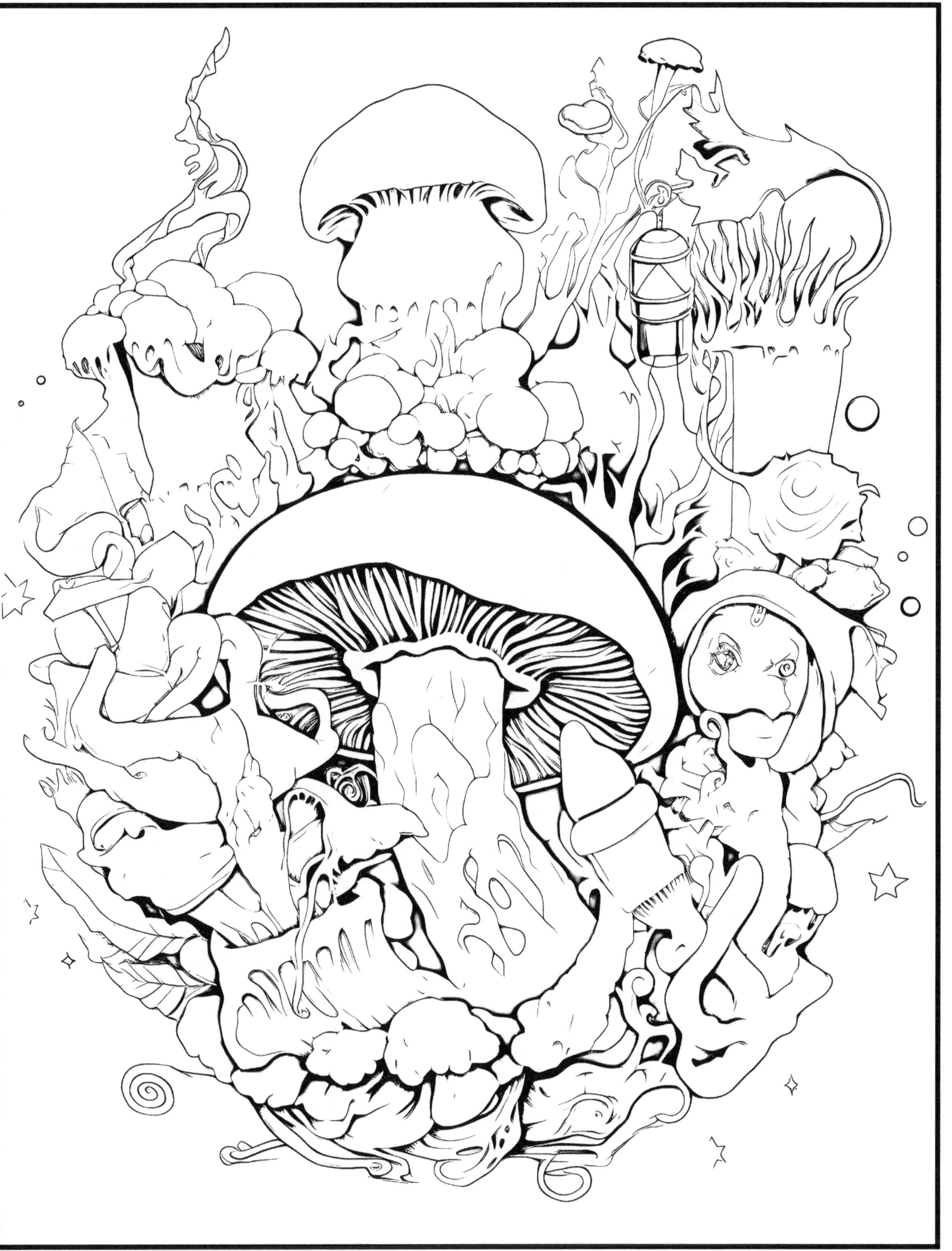

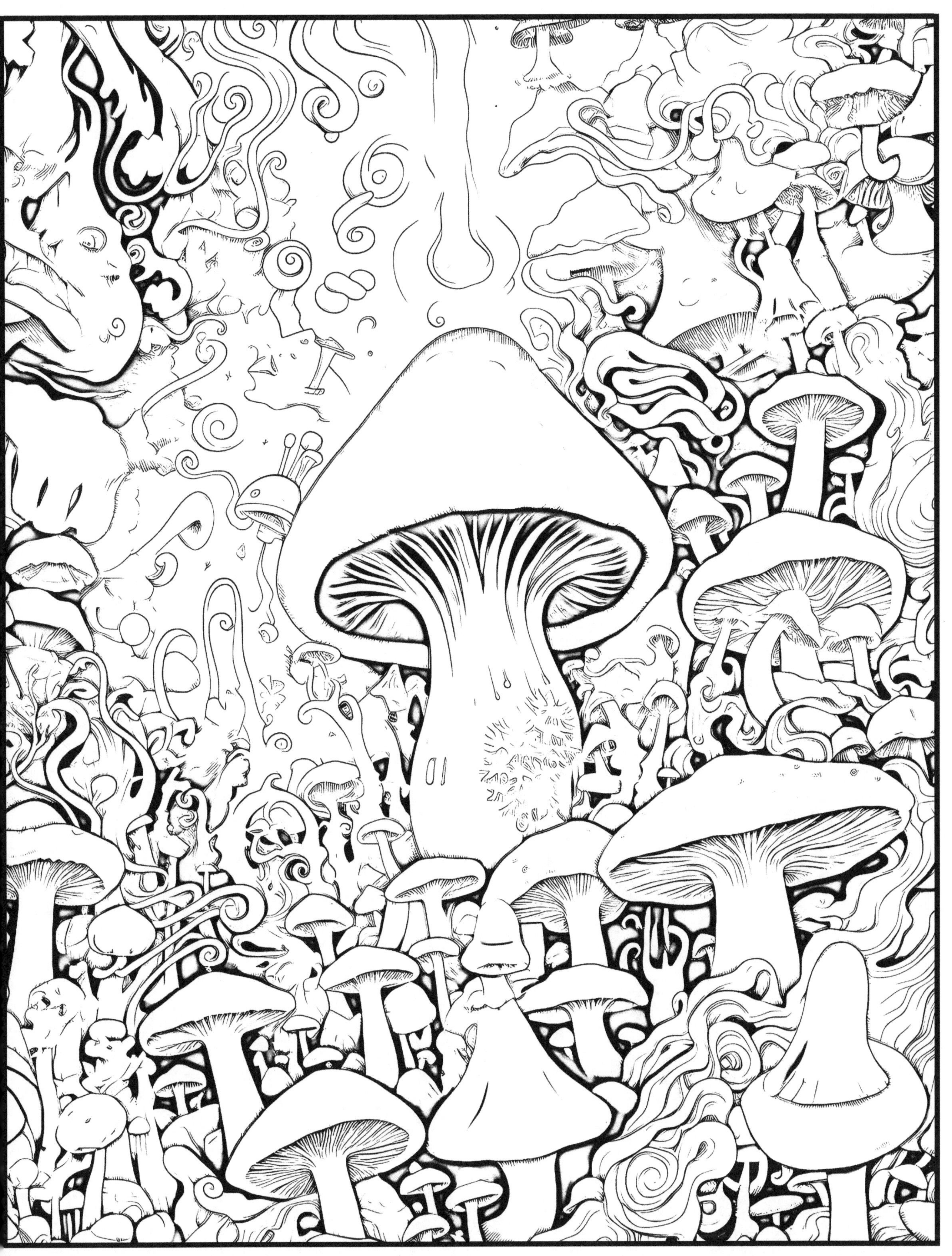

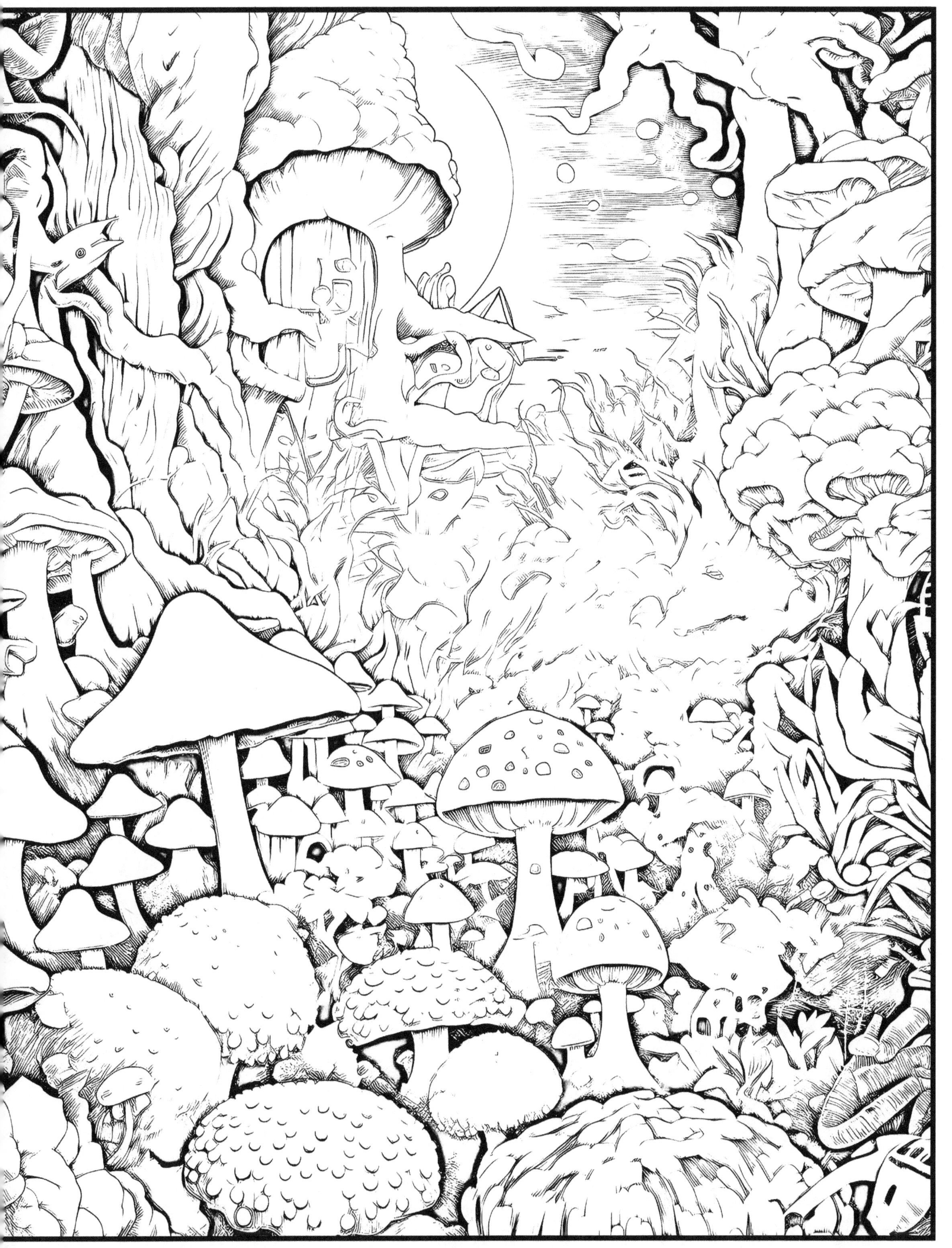

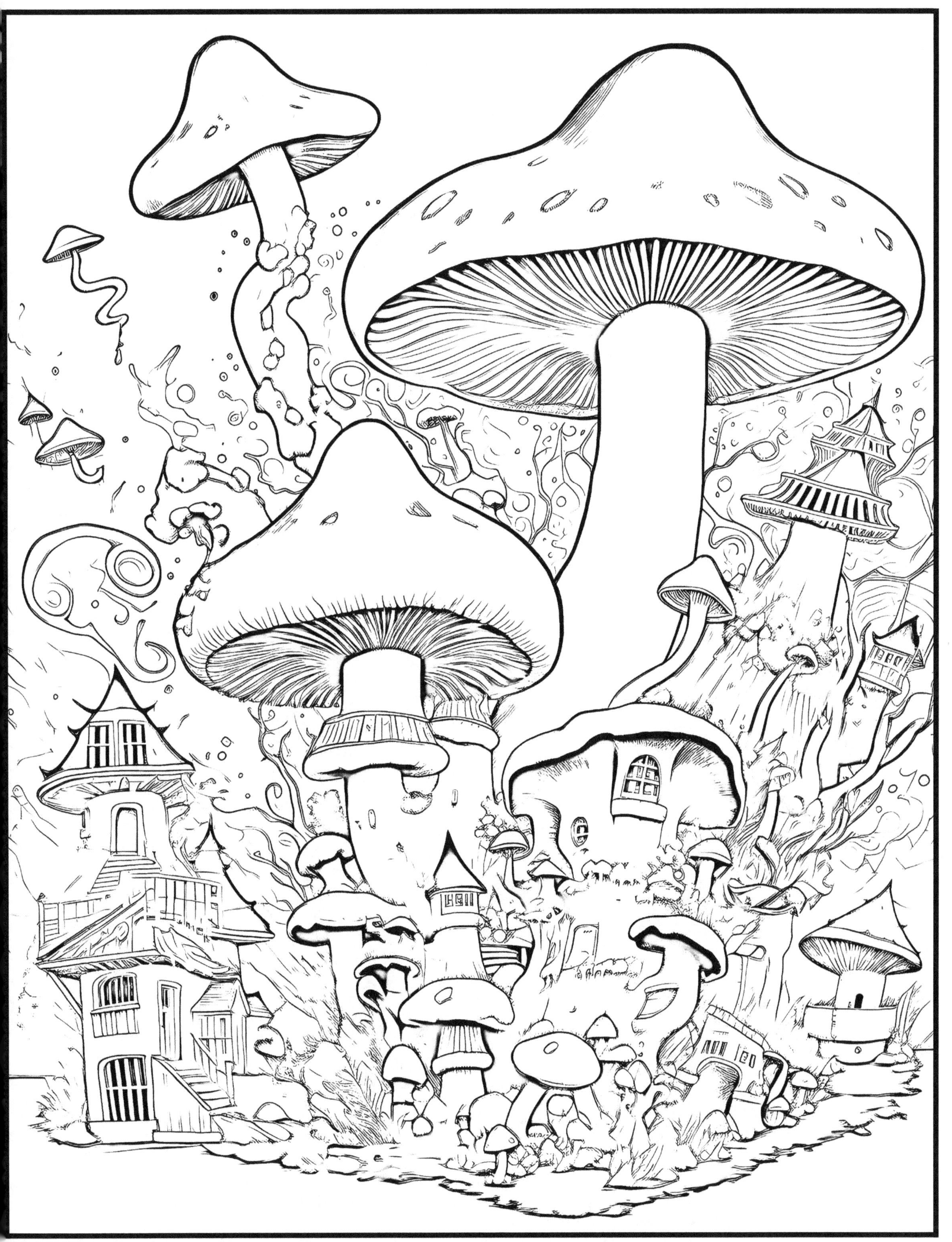

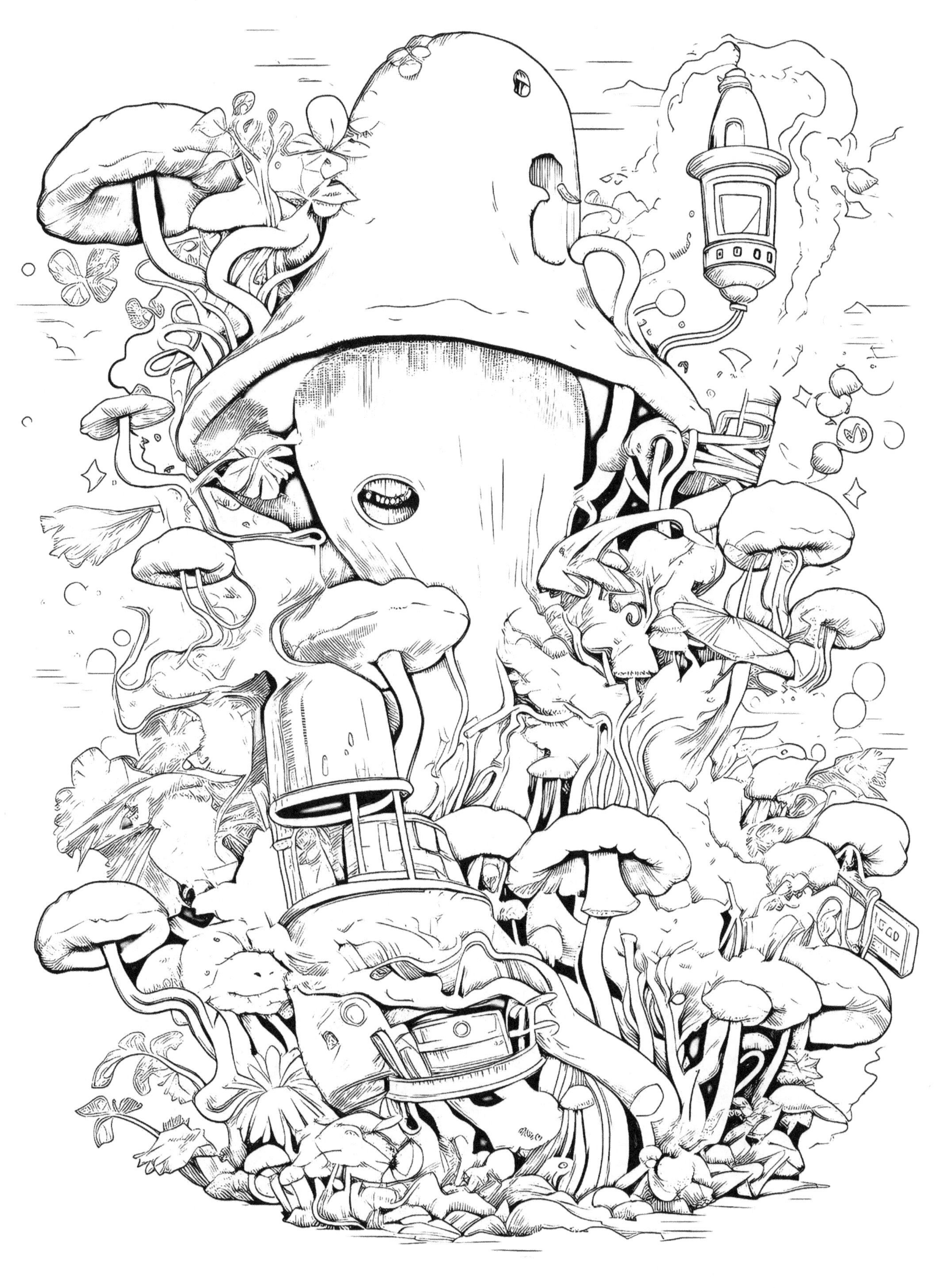

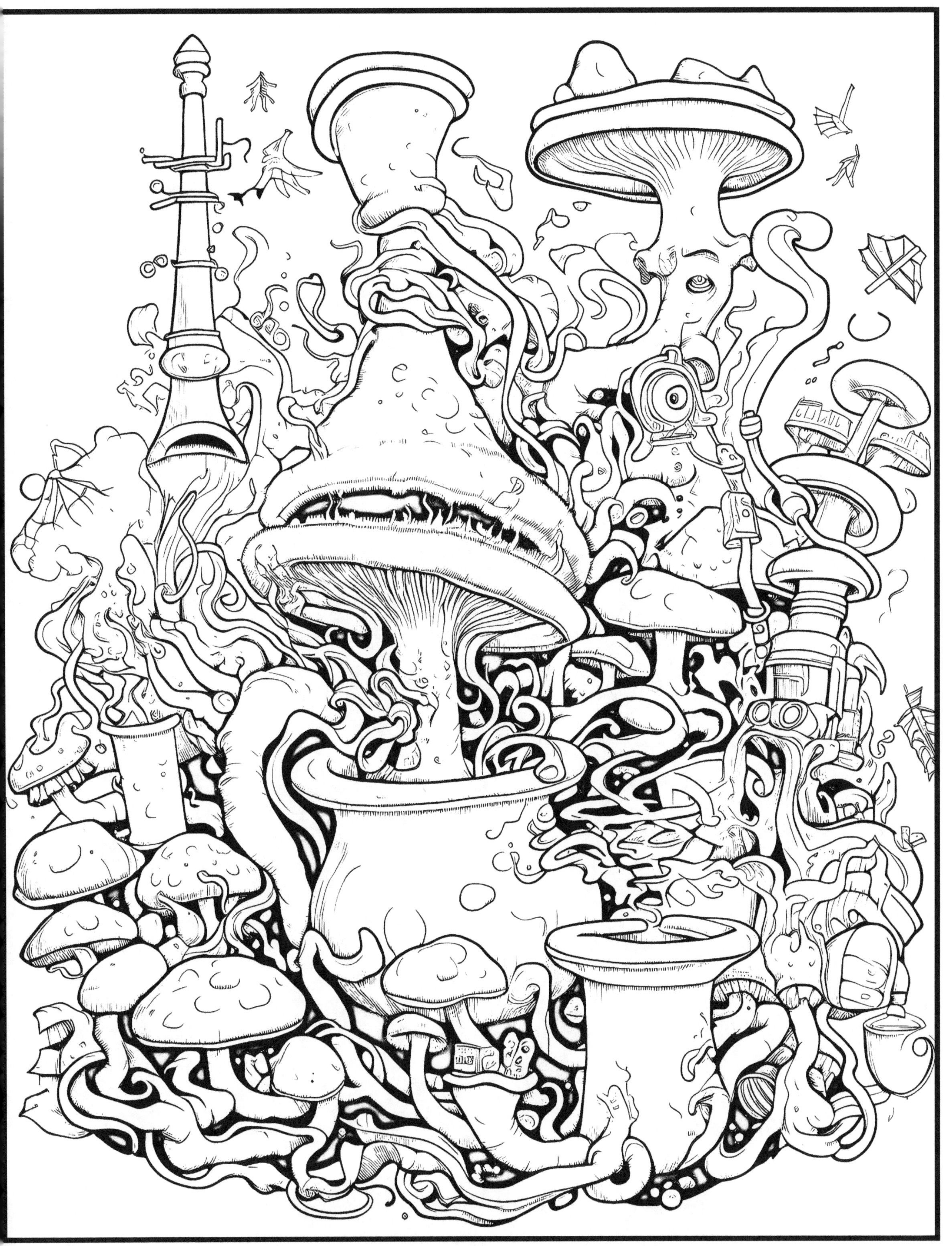

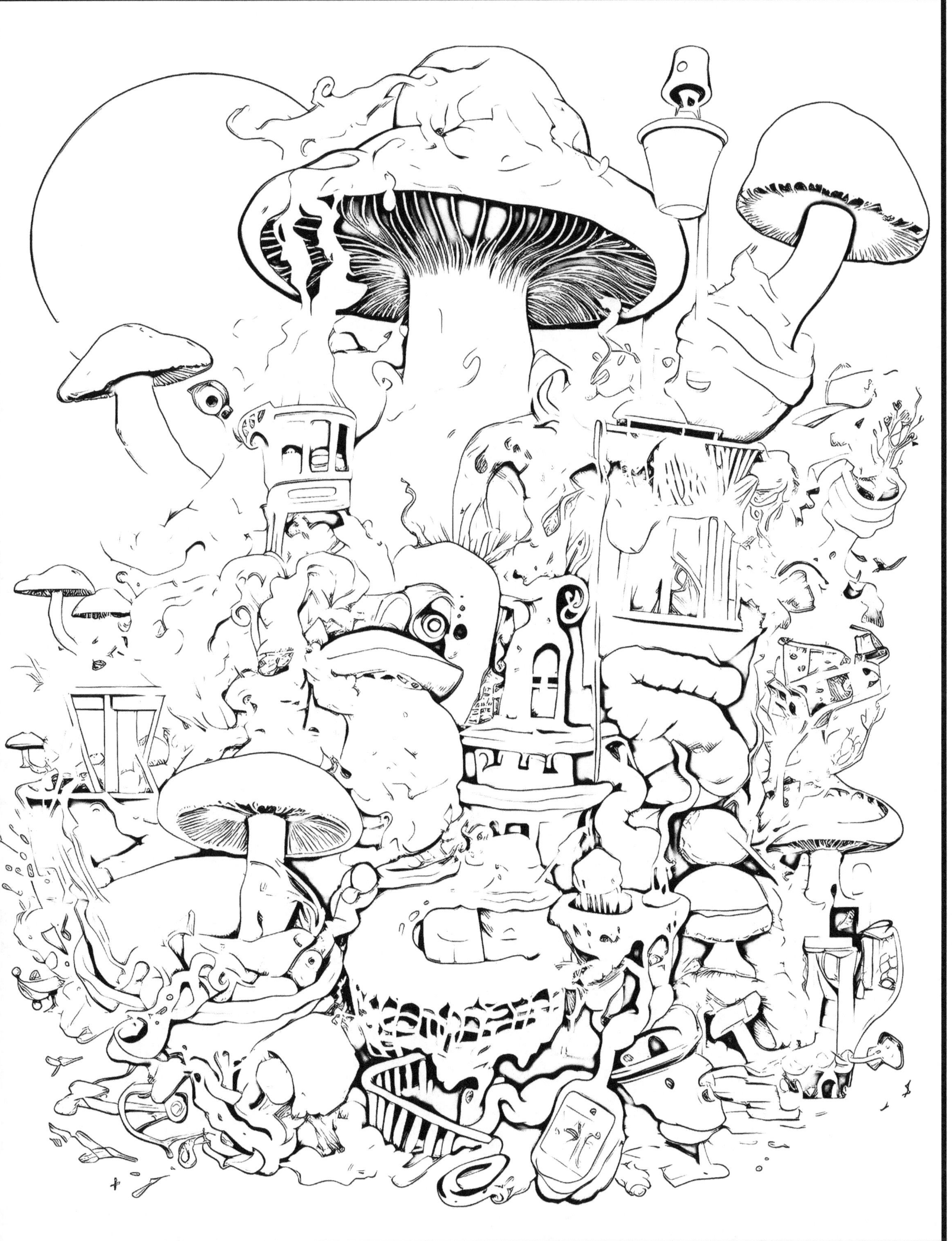

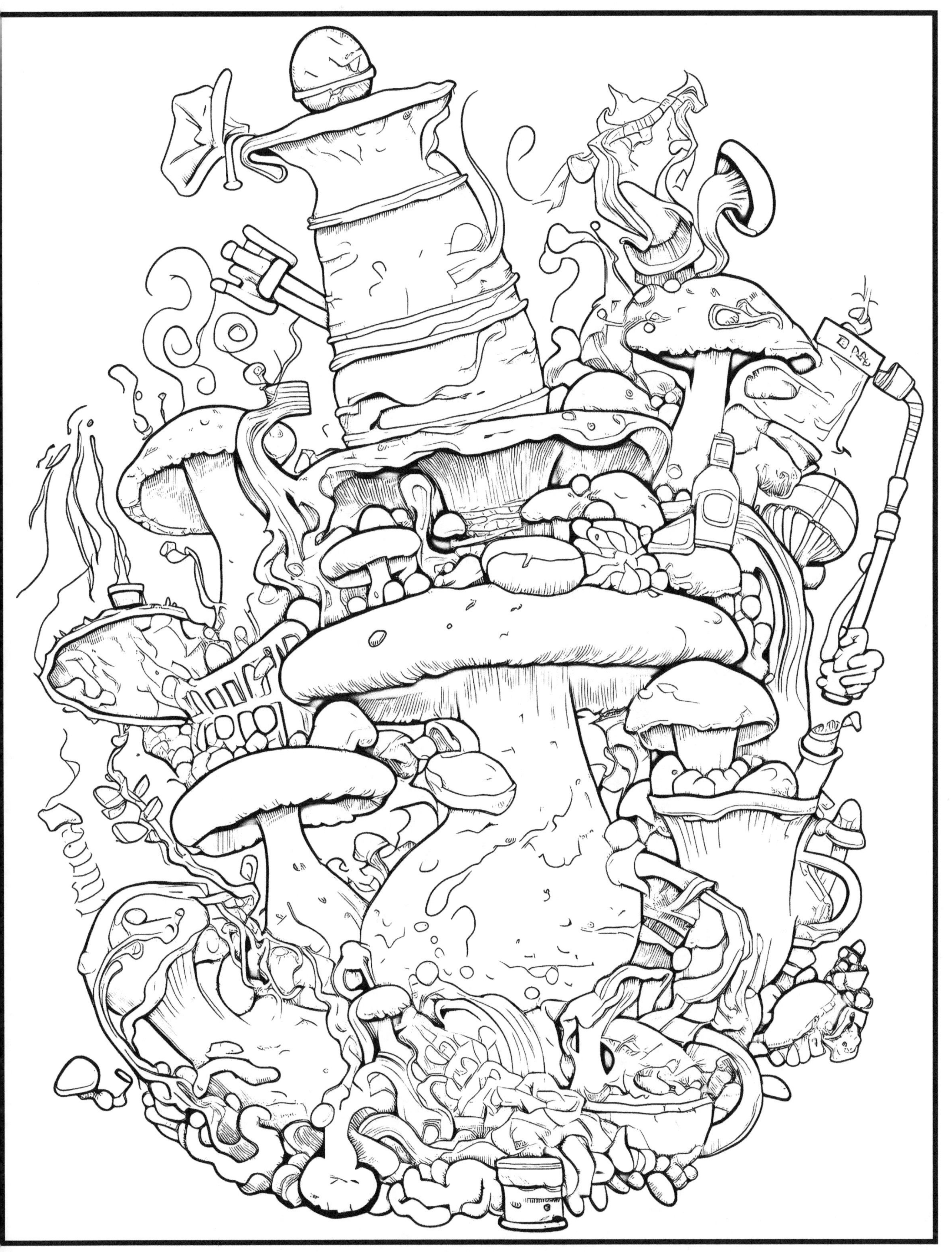

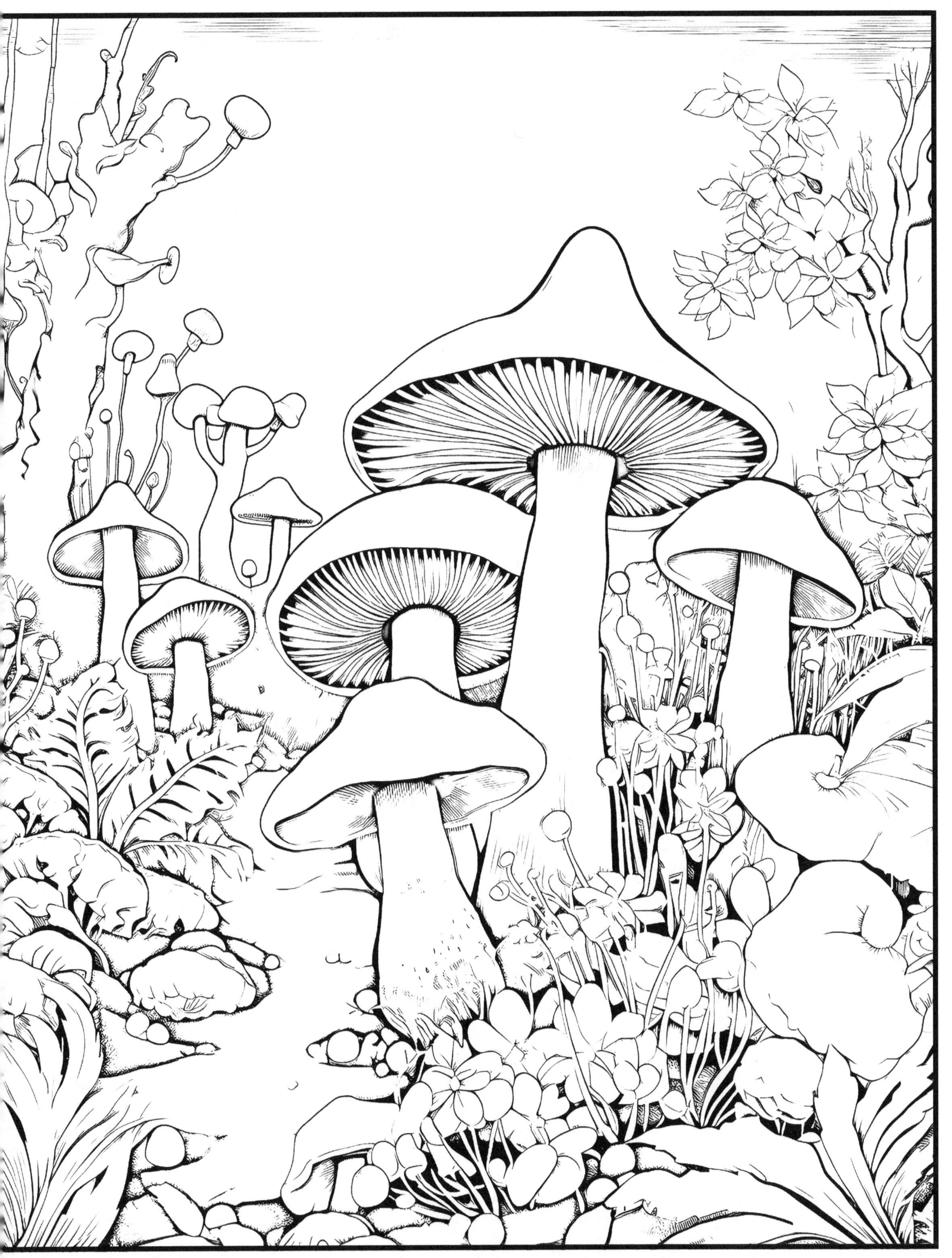

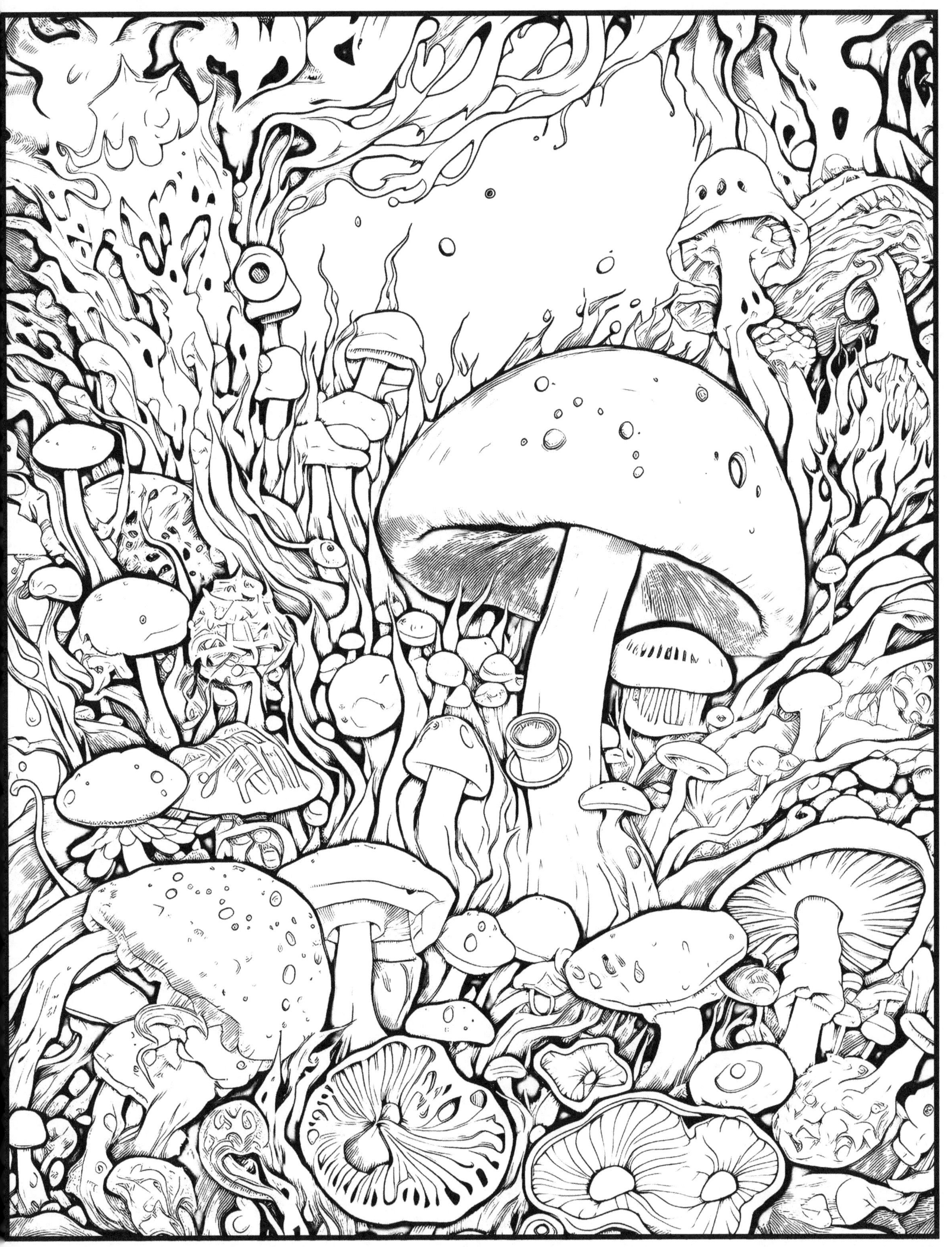

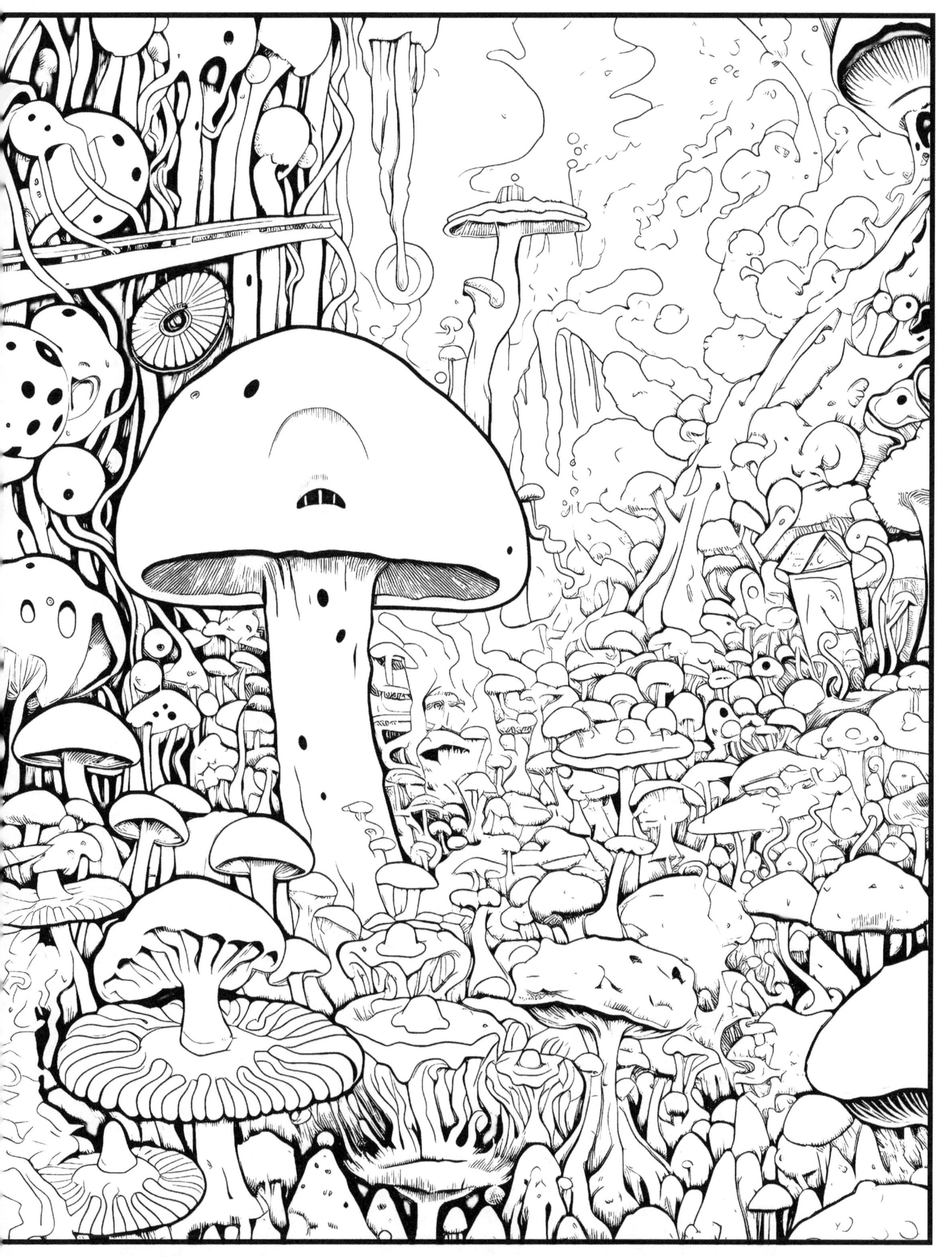

www.ingramcontent.com/pod-product-compliance
Lightning Source LLC
LaVergne TN
LVHW081424110826
845149LV00010B/1856
* 9 7 8 1 9 6 1 8 3 7 0 2 7 *